JUSTIN AND THE BULLY

written by Tony and Lauren Dungy
with Nathan Whitaker

illustrated by
Vanessa Brantley Newton

Ready-to-Read

Simon Spotlight
New York   London   Toronto   Sydney   New Delhi

To our children: Tiara, Jamie, Eric, Jordan, Jade, Justin, Jason, and Jalen —T. D. and L. D.

"Do to others as you would have them do to you."

—Luke 6:31 (NIV)

SIMON SPOTLIGHT
An imprint of Simon & Schuster Children's Publishing Division
1230 Avenue of the Americas, New York, New York 10020
Text copyright © 2012 by Tony Dungy and Lauren Dungy
Illustrations copyright © 2012 by Vanessa Brantley Newton
Published in association with the literary agency of Legacy, LLC, Winter Park, FL 32789
All rights reserved, including the right of reproduction in whole or in part in any form.
SIMON SPOTLIGHT, READY-TO-READ, and colophon are registered trademarks of Simon & Schuster, Inc.
For information about special discounts for bulk purchases, please contact Simon & Schuster Special
Sales at 1-866-506-1949 or business@simonandschuster.com.
The Simon & Schuster Speakers Bureau can bring authors to your live event. For more information or to
book an event contact the Simon & Schuster Speakers Bureau at 1-866-248-3049 or visit our website at
www.simonspeakers.com.
Manufactured in the United States of America 0816 LAK
10 9 8 7 6 5 4
Library of Congress Cataloging-in-Publication Data
Dungy, Tony.
Justin and the bully / by Tony and Lauren Dungy ; illustrated by Vanessa Brantley Newton. — 1st ed.
p. cm. — (Ready-to-read)
Summary: "Justin is thrilled to be on a soccer team. But at his very first practice, he is approached by a
tall girl who calls him "Shorty." She tells him he's too little to be on the team and that he should just go
home. Justin doesn't know what to do. He loves soccer, but he doesn't want to be teased"— Provided by
publisher.
[1. Soccer—Fiction. 2. Bullies—Fiction. 3. Size—Fiction. 4. Teamwork (Sports)—Fiction.] I. Dungy, Lauren.
II. Newton, Vanessa, ill. III. Title.
PZ7.D9187Jus 2012
[E]—dc23
2012024147
ISBN 978-1-4424-5718-8 (pbk)
ISBN 978-1-4424-5719-5 (hc)
ISBN 978-1-4424-5720-1 (eBook)

A NEW ADVENTURE

Justin loved soccer.
He loved to play at school.
He loved to play at the park.
Justin would play soccer
anywhere, anytime.

One day at the park, Justin saw a sign.
"Mom, look! Can I play? Please, Mom?
I've never been on a team before."
Mom smiled and said, "Okay!
Let's sign up."
Justin shouted, "Hooray!"

That afternoon Justin raced
all the way home.
He ran through the house
telling everyone the news.

"Jordan, guess what?
I get to play soccer!"
"That's great," said Jordan.
"You're good at kicking."

"Jade, guess what? I get to play soccer!"
"That's great," said Jade.
"You're really fast."

"Dad, guess what? I get to play soccer!"
"That's great," said Dad. "You'll be
a good teammate."

"Jason, guess what?
I get to play soccer!"
Jason smiled at his big brother
and clapped.
"Yay!" said Jason.

A ROUGH START

Justin went to his first practice
and met Coach Harris.
Coach Harris was very nice.
So were all of his teammates . . .
except for one.

Taylor wasn't friendly at all.
"Come here, Shorty!" said Taylor.
Justin looked around.
Who was Taylor talking to?

Taylor pointed at Justin. "I'm talking to you, Shorty!"

Justin looked to his left.

There was no one there.

Justin looked to his right.

There was no one there.

No one had ever called Justin "Shorty" before.

He thought Taylor must have been
talking to someone else.
But there was no one else around.
Taylor was talking to him.
Taylor walked closer to Justin.
She was very tall!
She leaned down and whispered to
him, "You're too little to play.
You should just go home, Shorty."

After soccer practice,
the car ride home was very quiet.
"Justin," Mom asked,
"did you have fun today?"
"I guess," Justin said and looked down
at his sneakers.

At dinner Dad asked Justin,
"How did your soccer practice go
today?
Did you have fun?"
"I don't think I want to play soccer
anymore," Justin blurted out.

Everybody looked surprised.
"But you love soccer," Dad said.
"And you were so excited,"
Mom said.

"I'm too small," Justin said.
"Everyone else is bigger than I am.
You've got to be big to play soccer."

"But you're good at kicking,"
Jade said.
"And you're so fast," Jordan said.
"But I'm not big enough,"
Justin said.
He looked very sad.

"Did the coach say you are too short?
Dad asked.
"No," Justin replied. "But Taylor did."

That night Mom and Dad went to
Justin's room to say good night.
"We'd like you to try soccer practice
one more time tomorrow."
"Okay," Justin agreed, but he still
seemed unhappy.

The next day Mom spoke
to Coach Harris.
"Justin doesn't want to play soccer
anymore. One of his teammates
told him he's too short," Mom said.
Coach Harris said, "Don't worry.
I know what to do."

The coach called the team together.
"We are a team," he said. "Right?"
Everyone said, "Right, Coach!"

"And on a good team there are no bullies. Right?"
"Right, Coach!" everybody said.

Then the coach asked,
"What is a bully?"
Everyone raised their hand
except for Taylor.

"Someone who acts mean,"
said Christophe.
"Someone who calls people names,"
said Grayson.
"Someone who pushes," said Nico.

"Those are all correct," said Coach Harris. "A bully tries to make someone else feel scared or bad. Bullying is wrong. We should never do it. Not to our teammates or anyone else."

"Is it right to help a bully be mean
to someone else?"
the coach asked the team.
"No!" everybody shouted.
Everybody but Taylor.
"Remember, treat others like you want
them to treat you," the coach said.

"I have a question," said Justin.
"Sure, Justin, what is it?"
asked Coach Harris.
"Is it time for soccer now?"
asked Justin.
"Yes, it is!" the coach said. "Let's go!"

Saturday was the first big game.
Everyone was excited,
and the team was playing great.
They scored a lot of goals,
and everybody was working hard
and having fun.

Logan had the ball.
"Don't kick it to Shorty Justin!
He's too little!" shouted Taylor.
Logan looked at Taylor and said,
"You're being a bully,
and bullying is never right."

Then Logan passed the ball
to Taylor. Justin ran fast
toward the goal, and Taylor saw him
close to the net.
Suddenly Taylor kicked the ball
to Justin!
Justin scored!
"Yay!" everybody yelled.

"Great teamwork out there today!"
the coach said after the game.
"I'm so proud of all of you!"
Taylor tapped Justin on the shoulder.
She was holding up her hand.
Justin gave Taylor a high five.
"Now we are a team!" they shouted.
And everyone cheered.